THIS
BOOK
BELONGS
TO

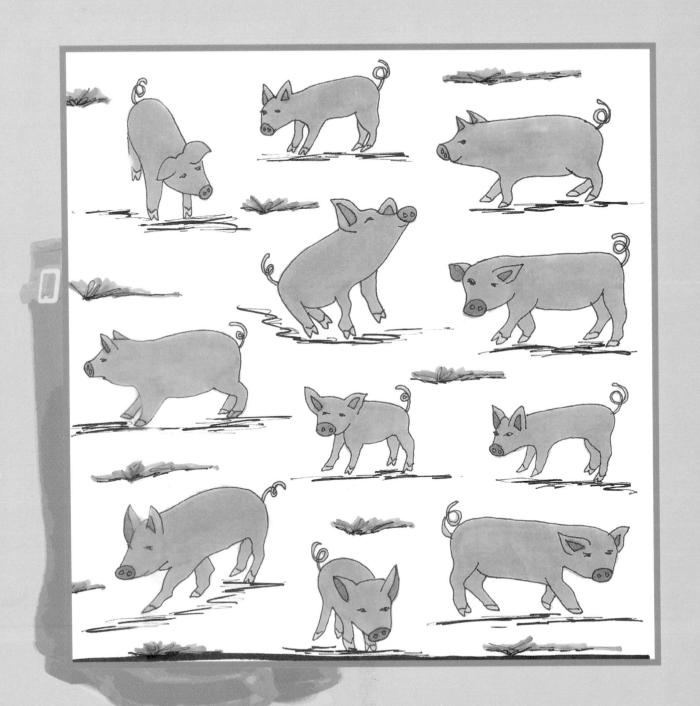

STORY FOUR
IN THE SERIES
'LIFE ON THE FARM'

AuthorHouse™
1663 Liberty Drive
Bloomington, IN 47403
www.authorhouse.com
Phone: 1-800-839-8640

First published by AuthorHouse 11/15/2011

ISBN: 978-1-4670-9803-8 (sc)

Library of Congress Control Number: 2011960753

Printed in the United States of America

Any people depicted in stock imagery provided by Thinkstock are models,
and such images are being used for illustrative purposes only.
Certain stock imagery © Thinkstock.

This book is printed on acid-free paper.

WRITTEN BY DOVIE G. THERRIAULT-BRUDER

ILLUSTRATED BY DOVIE G. THERRIAULT-BRUDER

MANY THANKS

TO ALL WHO PARTICIPATED

IN THE MAKING OF THIS BOOK

I WOULD LIKE TO DEDICATE THIS BOOK

TO MY GRAND-DAUGHTER ALEXA

"WHOSE LIKES AND DISLIKES" AT THE RIPE OLD AGE OF THREE!

HAVE INSPIRED ME TO WRITE ABOUT "MY DISLIKE" ABOUT LIFE
ON THE FARM

THANK YOU ALEXA

AND I HOPE YOU "LIKE" THIS LITTLE STORY!

ADVENTURE WITH THE PIGS

Shayna has lived on a farm with her parents for a total of nine years now.

She loves all the animals including the cows, the horses, the pigs, the sheep, the goats, the chickens, the geese, the rabbits, the cats *and* the dog.

She enjoys them all!

Shayna's mom likes them too, all except for the pigs! She enjoys waking up to all the animals chattering with each other. The very first thing in the morning, she hears the rooster crow.

"Cock-a-doodle-doo," he sings, "Cock-a-doodle-doo."

He wakes everyone up for breakfast with his very loud song.

"Cock-a-doodle-doo," he sings over and over again.

When breakfast is finished in the house, Shayna knows that the cats and the dog are sitting outside by the door waiting for their breakfast too. Shayna fills their food dishes and their water bowls.

She says good-morning to her cats Angel, Smartie and Mush. Then, she stoops to pet her dog Woofus.

From the house, Shayna hears the barnyard animals. The horses say 'neigh', the cows say 'moo', and the sheep say 'baa'.

She can hear the chickens in the chicken coop too.

"Bok-bok-bok-kok", they say, "Bok-bok-bok-kok".

Everyone on the farm is waking up and they all sound hungry!

Shayna and her mom walk down to the barn after breakfast to feed the rest of the animals.

They are always watching for the pesky pigs when they are outside.

The pigs are so very cute when they are little piglets but when they grow up, they are not very nice at all.

They are definitely not the favorite animal of Shayna's mom!

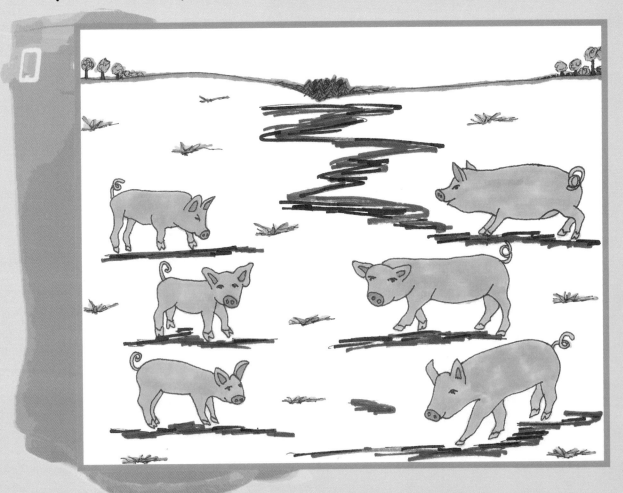

The problem with the pigs is that they just love dirt. Especially dirt with water on it! Yep, they just love mud! They can even smell it!

On their way to the barn, they see no rain clouds in the sky. It's been a few days now since the garden has had a drink and Shayna's mom is thinking that she needs to water it today.

Every time that she waters it, the pigs can somehow smell the cool, wet soil. They will head for the garden as fast as they can go.

They love to dig and lie down in the mud!

Shayna's mom notices the pigs on their way to the garden and she asks Shayna to come and help her to chase them away.

She waves her hands at them and hollers "Go piggies go! Go back to the barnyard, go!"

Together, they shout and wave franticly, and the pigs head back towards the barn.

Shayna and her mom continue on with the chores, making sure that all of the animals have food and water.

The pigs are very happy to receive their portions of grain and food scraps and they stay near the barn for awhile to enjoy their breakfast. Shayna thinks the pigs are the best composters ever because they eat up all the food scraps and they make fertilizer for the garden!

Woofus has tagged along for the morning chores and he sits nearby, watching the pigs eat.

He knows that they are not allowed to go by the house *or* by the garden.

He waits patiently for them to finish eating and make their move.

With all of the animals fed, and the sprinkler going on the garden, Shayna and her mom go back to the house.

Woofus comes along with them, but stops near the garden to protect it. He knows that the pigs will come to root as soon as they smell the mud.

He knows his duty well and he sits to wait for them.

He also loves to run and chase the pigs back to the barn!

"Shayna, would you like some lemonade?" her mom asks.

"Lemonade sounds like a great idea!" she answers.

Her mom goes inside to make some juice and Shayna sits on the step to watch for those pesky pigs.

After a while, she sees them coming. She bolts from the step to help Woofus herd them away from the garden and back to the barn.

"Go piggies go", she yells. "Go back to the barnyard. Go!"

Off they run squealing, with their tails down.

Shayna stoops to pet Woofus who is wagging his tail happily!

"Good boy", she says. "Good dog."

Her mom opens the door and calls her from the steps.

"The lemonade is ready," she says.

They drink a cool glass of juice while sitting on the step enjoying the sunshine.

"You're going to have a busy day today keeping those pesky pigs out of the garden Shayna", her mom says.

"I know," says Shayna laughing.

She loves the chase just as much as Woofus does!

Her mom takes the lemonade glasses back inside and Shayna keeps watch over the garden from the steps.

After a bit, she decides to go and play with Woofus.

They run and tumble on the grass and are having a great time!

Before they realize it, the pigs are on the edge of the garden ready to step into the mud. Shayna yells and Woofus barks! The chase is on!

"Go piggies go. Go back to the barnyard. Go!" Shayna yells.

Off they run, back to the barn as fast as their short little legs can carry them!

Shayna's mom has stayed inside to clean up the breakfast dishes.

Shayna does not get to help with the dishes today because she has a much more important job to do.

Her job, today, is to help Woofus keep the pigs out of the garden!

As her mom watches out the window, she is also thinking. She is thinking about those pesky pigs and why they love to get into her garden when it is wet!

The only reason that she can think of is that they just love the mud!

"*Ah, the pigs love the mud!*" she says out loud.

Now, she has an idea! She heads outside to talk with Shayna about what she is thinking.

They smile at each other and head for the barn.

They tell Woofus to guard the garden from the pesky pigs and he does!

At the barn, Shayna's mom goes inside and brings out a shovel for herself and a bucket for Shayna.

Together, Shayna and her mom go around to the back of the barn. Shayna's mom finds a spot with no grass and lots of dirt. She begins to dig up the soil and put in into a pile.

She sends Shayna to get water from the creek which is just a short walk from where she is digging. Shayna brings a full bucket of water. She dumps it where her mom tells her to dump it.

They continue on with 'digging' and 'dumping' until it is past lunch time.

A few times, they can hear Woofus barking. They know that he is chasing the pigs because they can hear them squealing!

Shayna's mom is thinking that it looks really wet and muddy, so she steps back and begins to call the pesky pigs.

"Come piggies come," she calls.

Shayna joins in, calling "Come piggies come."

Around the corner they come! They head right into the newly made mud puddle!

Shayna and her mom laugh and laugh. The pigs grunt and snort a big 'THANK-YOU'.

"No more pesky pigs in my garden!" Shayna's mom says.

"Nope," said Shayna with a big smile.

I just love all of the adventure on the farm, she thinks, and my mom is sooo smart!

THE END

THANK YOU

FOR READING MY STORIES

IN THE SERIES

I CALL

'LIFE ON THE FARM'

CPSIA information can be obtained
at www.ICGtesting.com
Printed in the USA
260183LV00002B

9781467098038